"Somebody Stole My Cat."

Startled, the judge looked at Rosie and said, "What?"

"My cat's gone. Somebody stole him."

"Aren't you the girl with the sandy beach, in the Domestic House Cat category?"

"Yes. My cat is Webster and he's gone." Rosie's voice got louder each time she said the terrible words.

"Shhh," said one of the other judges.

"I'll talk to you after the Parade of Champions ends," the first judge said. "Why would anyone steal a house cat?"

Rosie felt tears forming. She didn't know why. All she knew was that Webster was gone. Now it was up to Rosie and Kayo to get him back. She turned and ran out of the gymnasium. . . .

Books by Peg Kehret

Cages
Horror at the Haunted House
Nightmare Mountain
Sisters, Long Ago
Terror at the Zoo
Frightmares: Cat Burglar on the Prowl

Available from MINSTREL Books

FRIGHTMARES™

Cat Burglar on the Prowl

Peg Kehret

To Kiel Petersen
Happy reading

Peg Kehret

A
MINSTREL® BOOK

PUBLISHED BY POCKET BOOKS

New York   London   Toronto   Sydney   Tokyo   Singapore

This book is a work of fiction. Names, characters, places, and incidents are products of the author's imagination or are used fictitiously. Any resemblance to actual events or locales or persons, living or dead, is entirely coincidental.

A MINSTREL PAPERBACK *ORIGINAL*

A Minstrel Book published by
POCKET BOOKS, a division of Simon & Schuster Inc.
1230 Avenue of the Americas, New York, NY 10020

Copyright © 1995 by Peg Kehret

ISBN: 0-671-89187-1

First Minstrel Books paperback printing January 1995

10 9 8 7 6 5 4 3 2 1

FRIGHTMARES is a trademark of Simon & Schuster, Inc.

A MINSTREL BOOK and colophon are registered trademarks of Simon & Schuster Inc.

Cover art by Dan Burr

Printed in the U.S.A.

*For all the book store owners
who give new writers a chance,
especially Magda Hitzroth*

CARE CLUB
We Care About Animals

I. Whereas we, the undersigned, care about our animal friends, we promise to groom them, play with them, and exercise them daily. We will do this for the following animals:

> **WEBSTER** (Rosie's cat)
> **BONE BREATH** (Rosie's dog)
> **HOMER** (Kayo's cat)
> **DIAMOND** (Kayo's cat)

II. Whereas we, the undersigned, care about the well-being of *all* creatures, we promise to do whatever we can to help homeless animals.

III. Care Club will hold official meetings every Thursday afternoon or whenever else there is important business. All Care Club projects will be for the good of the animals.

Signed:

Rosie Saunders

Kayo Benton

Chapter

1

$\mathcal{T}$he cats did not come to greet her that day.

Kayo Benton arrived home from school at the usual time, but when she slipped her key into the apartment door lock and clicked it to the right, the sound failed to bring Homer and Diamond running.

Kayo glanced through the day's mail as she pushed the door open, hoping the free pamphlet she had sent for, *World Series Facts*, would be there. When it wasn't, she tossed the mail on the small table just inside the front door and looked around for Homer and Diamond.

Usually, they wound themselves around her ankles before she could get in the door, telling her they had missed her and it was time to be fed. Not necessarily in that order.

"I'm home," she called, but neither cat appeared.

Odd, Kayo thought. Were they sick?

Kayo hurried down the bedroom hallway. Homer and Diamond always slept on her bed, ignoring the two cat baskets, complete with pillows, that Kayo provided for them.

In the doorway of her bedroom she stopped. Apprehension whispered up her spine.

The contents of her dresser drawers had been dumped in a pile on her bed. The shoes had been flung from her closet, her pillow was on the floor, and the cushion of the small blue chair in the corner was tipped up, as if someone had looked underneath it.

Someone's been here, she realized. Someone has searched my room.

"Diamond?" she said. "Homer? Come, kitty, kitty, kitty."

A low meow came from under the bed. Kayo dropped to her knees, lifted the bedspread, and looked. Both cats stared back at her, apparently unharmed. She called them again, but they remained huddled together in the far corner.

Kayo got up and ran to her mother's bedroom, to use the telephone. Goose bumps rose on her arms as she entered. Every drawer had been emptied on the bed. The sweaters and sweatshirts that Kayo's mom kept on the shelf in her closet had been thrown on the floor. And the musical jewelry box lay on its side on top of the dresser, with both trays empty.

Kayo dialed quickly. When the familiar voice answered, "Farley and Associates," Kayo cried, "Mom! We've been robbed!" Then she sank down on the edge of the bed, her legs suddenly shaky.

"I'll be right home," Mrs. Benton said. "Don't touch anything; the police will want to see what's happened. I'll call them now. If they get there before I do, be sure you look through the peephole and see their identification before you let them in."

"I will," Kayo said.

As soon as she hung up, Kayo raced back to her own room. She opened the battered old toy box that she'd had since she was two, and sighed with relief.

Her baseball card collection was still there. She lifted out the top album, opened it, and flipped through the pages, just to make sure. The faces of the 1989 Atlanta Braves smiled at her, followed by the Baltimore Orioles and the Boston White Sox.

Kayo looked quickly around her room. Her baseball bat stood in the corner; her baseball caps, sixteen of them, hung from the pegboard on the wall. Her glove was in its usual place on top of her dresser. Nothing was missing. Of course, except for her baseball cards, she didn't own anything valuable. While the caps were treasures to Kayo, most had been purchased for fifty cents or less at garage sales or thrift shops, and a thief wouldn't give them a second glance.

Thank goodness the thief had not looked in her toy box. Probably, she decided, thieves know that kids don't hide large sums of money or valuable jewels in a toy box.

Kayo lay on the floor beside her bed and talked softly to the cats, coaxing them out. Her orange-and-white cat, Diamond, emerged first, slinking slowly forward to sniff Kayo's fingers. Kayo scooped Diamond up and rubbed her cheek against the soft fur, trying to calm her shattered nerves.

"Did you see him?" she whispered. "Do you know who was here?" Diamond meowed and struggled out of Kayo's arms, more interested in food than in cuddling. When Homer, the gray-striped cat, heard cat food being poured into the bowls, he came out, too, complaining noisily.

Kayo stayed in her bedroom, petting the cats while they ate. She wondered what the thieves might have taken from the rest of the apartment, but she didn't go look. She just sat on the rug beside Homer and Diamond and waited.

The cats were still eating their crunchies when she heard a sound at the front door. Kayo's heart began to race. It was too soon for her mom to be home; Mrs. Benton rode the bus to work, and even if she didn't have to wait for a bus, it was a fifteen-minute ride and then a two-block walk from the bus stop to their apartment.

The police would knock, wouldn't they? They wouldn't try to come in.

Had she locked the door after she got home, as she was supposed to? Usually, she did it automatically, but today she had been thinking about the *World Series Facts* pamphlet and wondering where the cats were. Had she forgotten to turn the dead bolt? Kayo couldn't remember.

Homer and Diamond heard the door, too, and stopped eating. Instead of strolling out to the front hall to act as the welcoming committee, which they usually seemed to think was their responsibility, both cats ran back under Kayo's bed.

"Kayo? It's me!"

At the sound of her mother's voice, relief

surged through Kayo and she ran to the door. "How did you get here so fast?" she asked.

"I took a cab."

Mrs. Benton *never* took a cab. Even when it snowed and the walk to the bus was hazardous, she refused to spend the extra money.

"The police haven't come yet," Kayo said.

"They said it might be an hour or so, since no one is in danger."

While they waited for the police to come, Kayo and Mrs. Benton walked through the rest of their apartment.

"The TV is gone," Kayo said. "How am I going to watch the World Series?"

When they reached the small sideboard in the dining room, Mrs. Benton burst into tears.

"My tea set," she cried. "They took Grandmother Kearney's silver tea set."

Kayo had seen her mother cry only once before—the day she told Kayo about the divorce.

Waves of frustration washed over Kayo, and she brushed tears from her own eyes. It wasn't fair! The silver tea set meant nothing to the thief; it would be sold, maybe even melted down, and it was the only family heirloom Mrs. Benton had.

Kayo knew its history by heart. When Mrs. Benton's Grandfather and Grandmother Kearney were newly married, they raised Jersey cattle.

They borrowed money to take their prize cow, Clara Mae, to the State Fair, and to their everlasting delight, Clara Mae was declared the Grand Champion. The prize was a silver tea set.

When Grandfather Kearney said they would have to sell the tea set to get the money to repay their loan, Grandmother Kearney refused. Instead, she went door to door all winter, selling eggs from her chickens, until she had enough to repay what they had borrowed.

Mrs. Benton remembered the silver tea set, polished until it gleamed, and in the place of honor on her grandparents' table. It was there when Mrs. Benton was a child; it was there when her grandparents died.

Kayo was not yet born when her Great-grandfather and Great-grandmother Kearney died, but the silver tea set had been displayed in her home as far back as she could remember, still polished, and still treasured. And now it was gone.

The thief also took Mrs. Benton's clock radio, a calculator, and the cash from an envelope marked "Grocery Money" that Mrs. Benton kept in the kitchen. She began a list of what was missing.

"It was all costume jewelry," Mrs. Benton told the police officer who arrived later, "but some pieces have sentimental value."

"How much cash is missing?" the officer asked.

"Only about six dollars. It's almost the end of the month."

For once, Kayo was glad her mother had little cash. Usually, the perpetual lack of money was a source of dismay, but now she felt some satisfaction in knowing that the burglar did not get away with a huge sum.

"Do you think it was the cat burglar we've been reading about?" Mrs. Benton asked.

"He usually works at night," the officer said, "but this is exactly how he leaves things: drawers dumped and cupboards open. Do you know how the thief got in? This door has not been forced open; could it have been unlocked?"

"I'm positive I locked the door when I left this morning," Mrs. Benton said.

"It was locked when I got home," Kayo said. "I heard it click when I turned the key and wondered why Homer and Diamond didn't come. The thief must have scared them; they were hiding under my bed when I got here, and they've acted spooked ever since."

The sliding door that went from the dining room to a small patio and yard was closed and locked, too. The wooden stick that Mrs. Benton kept in the track was in place. The door would not slide open unless the stick was removed.

"What about windows?" the officer asked. "Could there have been a window left unlocked? Or one with a broken latch?"

Mrs. Benton and Kayo looked at each other in dismay.

"Oh, no," Mrs. Benton said.

"The bathroom," Kayo said.

Mrs. Benton nodded. "My three-year-old nephew locked himself in the bathroom last week and wouldn't come out," she explained. "I forced the bathroom window open, and Kayo crawled through to get him. I meant to replace the window lock, but I hadn't done it yet."

They all trooped into the bathroom. A light breeze fluttered the curtains; the window was wide open.

"Looks like you made it easy for him," the officer said. "Be glad you weren't home."

Kayo shuddered.

"It makes me furious," Mrs. Benton said, "to think of a stranger pawing through my things, taking whatever he wanted. That tea set is eighty years old."

"You aren't the only victims," the officer said. "He robbed two other apartments in this same building. One person had left the door unlocked.

In the other apartment the thief lifted the sliding door to the patio out of its track."

The officer asked a few more questions, and Mrs. Benton signed a statement of what was missing. "You may discover that other items are gone," he said as he handed Mrs. Benton a business card. "If you do, let me know."

After he left, Kayo and her mother went to a hardware store and bought a new lock for the bathroom window. They went home, installed it, and then cleaned up the mess, putting everything back where it belonged. They worked silently, each absorbed in her own thoughts.

Kayo could think of nothing except the burglary. Hoping some music would distract her, she reached for her portable radio. It was gone. "Mom!" she cried. "He stole my radio!"

That night neither Kayo nor her mother could get to sleep. They sat up until midnight, eating popcorn and reading, unable to relax. Twice, they double-checked all the windows and the door, but the apartment seemed full of creaks and whispers.

"We can't even watch an old movie," Kayo complained. "That stupid cat burglar took our television set."

At one A.M. Kayo finally went to bed and drifted into an uneasy slumber. She knew the thief would not return. Why would he? He had already taken everything he wanted. Even so, Kayo jerked awake once and lay looking at the darkness, straining to hear any unusual sound.

Beside her, Homer twitched in his sleep, growling softly. Smiling at the idea of cat dreams, Kayo stroked his fur and turned on her side, bending her knees to make a cozy enclosure for Homer. He purred and licked her hand.

When the alarm rang the next morning, Kayo was glad to get up, even though she felt as if she had already run fifty laps. She wondered if she would ever relax again.

Chapter

"Why didn't you call me?" Rosie Saunders stood on the Oakwood School steps, hands on her hips and brown eyes flashing behind her glasses.

"What could you have done?" Kayo asked.

"I could have come over and cried with you. I could have stamped my feet and had a temper tantrum. I could have taken up a collection from our friends so you'd have money to buy food."

"He didn't take our food."

"Well, I could have done something."

"Mom and I were sort of in shock," Kayo said. "It was so awful, we just didn't feel like talking to anybody."

"Not even me? Best friends are supposed to tell each other when something important happens."

"I'm telling you now. I haven't told anyone else, except the police."

"I hope they catch him and lock him up for the rest of his life," Rosie said. "Your mom was crazy about that old teapot."

"At least he didn't take my baseball cards."

"Maybe Homer and Diamond saved them."

"What do you mean?" Kayo asked.

"Maybe the thief was getting ready to steal your baseball cards and the cats saw him and growled, and the thief was afraid they would attack him, so he left."

"Maybe they *did* attack him," Kayo said. "They were hiding under the bed when I got home, and last night Homer had a bad dream. Maybe they fought the thief!"

"If it weren't for Homer and Diamond," Rosie said, "those baseball cards might be gone."

The girls walked on toward their sixth-grade classroom.

"Let's have an extra Care Club meeting after school today," Rosie said. "If Homer and Diamond saved your baseball card collection, they deserve some special attention."

"Good idea. Besides, I have important new business to bring up. I got so upset about the robbery, I almost forgot about it."

"What is it?"

Before Kayo could answer, Sammy Hulenback joined them. "I hear you got robbed by the cat burglar," Sammy said.

"How did you find out?"

"My aunt works at the police station. She says sometimes cat burglars go back and rob the same house again."

"Thanks a lot, Sammy," Rosie said. "That's exactly what Kayo needs to hear right now."

"Just trying to help," Sammy said.

The bell rang. The kids quickly took their seats. Mrs. Cushman read the morning announcements and the students recited the Pledge of Allegiance. Kayo heard none of it. All she heard were Sammy's words, repeating themselves in her mind: *Sometimes cat burglars go back and rob the same house again.*

When she got home that afternoon, Kayo didn't want to go inside. It had never bothered her before to let herself in after school, even though her mother didn't get home until almost six. Kayo enjoyed the independence and the responsibility of feeding Homer and Diamond and scooping out their litter box. Sometimes Mrs. Benton left a note, asking Kayo to put potatoes in to bake or to do some other chore.

That first day after the robbery Kayo stood nervously outside her own front door with the key in her hand, thinking about an unknown person standing in her room, going through the contents of her drawers. Maybe she would wait until Rosie arrived for the Care Club meeting, and they could go in together.

I may never relax again, Kayo thought. My career as the first female pitcher in major league baseball will be cut short because I'll have a nervous breakdown.

The telephone rang. Quickly Kayo turned the key, opened the door, and hurried to answer. She nearly tripped over Homer and Diamond, who had come to greet her.

"Hi," Mrs. Benton said. "Just checking to be sure you're okay."

"Rosie's coming over," Kayo said. "We're having an extra Care Club meeting this week."

"Good." Kayo heard the relief in her mother's voice and realized Mom didn't want her home alone today.

Until Kayo started sixth grade, she had gone to a baby-sitter's every day after school. She didn't want to do that again. Forcing herself to sound cheerful, she said, "Everything's fine, Mom. Thanks for calling."

Rosie was ten minutes late for the Care Club meeting. She arrived out of breath, with a rusty red wagon tied behind her bicycle. A portable television set, wrapped in an old blanket, rode in the wagon.

"Where are you going with that?" Kayo asked.

"It's for you. Because yours got stolen." Rosie put her kickstand down, pulled off the blanket, and lifted the TV out of the wagon.

"Where did you get it?" Kayo asked.

"From one of our guest bedrooms. The one with the pea soup wallpaper. Mom says nobody ever turns this set on and it's just in the way so you might as well have it."

Kayo held the door open as Rosie carried the TV in and set it on the empty cart where the stolen set used to sit. It almost didn't fit, since the set Rosie brought was larger than the one that got stolen.

"That's an expensive TV," Kayo said. "I'm not sure Mom will let you give it to us."

"I am not lugging it back home," Rosie said. "It was all I could do to get it here. Do you know how hard it is to pump uphill pulling a heavy wagon? Besides, we still have four other television sets; how many TVs do three people need?"

"When your brother is home from college, there are four people."

"He has his own set. And my dad never watches TV, anyway."

"Thanks for bringing this one over," Kayo said. "Mom said we couldn't afford to buy another one for at least a month, which means I was going to miss the entire World Series."

"It was Mom's U.K. for today."

Kayo knew that Rosie's mother tried to do one unexpected kindness each day. "Tell your mom thanks," she said.

Rosie plopped down on the living room floor and took her dictionary out of her backpack. Her red T-shirt had a quote from Groucho Marx: *Outside of a dog, books are man's best friend. Inside of a dog, it's too dark to read.* "I still don't have a vocabulary word for this week," Rosie said.

Kayo opened her box of cat-grooming supplies and removed a steel comb. She sat down, with Homer in her lap, and began to comb him. Homer purred and kneaded Kayo's jeans with his claws. Diamond lay with her front paws tucked under her chest and watched.

"The Care Club meeting will now come to order," said Kayo.

Rosie paged through her dictionary.

"Is there a treasurer's report?" Kayo asked.

"We're broke, as always," said Rosie. She flipped a few pages of the dictionary.

"I have some important new business that might solve our financial problem," Kayo said. "The Cat Fanciers Association is having a cat show, and I think we should take Homer, Webster, and Diamond."

"Ineffable!" cried Rosie.

Homer twitched his tail. Kayo rubbed behind Homer's ears to soothe him.

Rosie read from the dictionary. " 'Ineffable: Incapable of being described in words.' " Rosie grinned. "What a great word," she said as she removed the small notebook and pencil that she always carried in her back pocket and wrote: *ineffable*. "It can mean something truly wonderful or something horrid."

"Will the meeting *please* come to order?" Kayo said. Usually, Rosie's determination to add one new word to her vocabulary every week—and to use the new word at least five times daily in ordinary conversation—was fun. But today Kayo wanted to get on with the meeting.

"It would be ineffable to win the lottery," said Rosie. "On the other hand, it was ineffable for you to be robbed by the cat burglar."

Kayo did not want to think about the cat burglar. "This is supposed to be a Care Club meeting," she complained, "not a marathon reading of the dictionary. I brought up some official new business, and I bet you don't even know what it is."

"Yes, I do. You want to take Homer and Diamond and Webster to see a cat show."

"Not to watch. I want to enter them in the cat show."

"Cat shows only take purebred cats with long names like Princess Flaxenhair of Purrsylvania. You need official certified papers that prove your cat is a direct descendant of Abraham Lincoln's cat, or her ancestors were pets of the Pilgrims."

"This cat show is different." Kayo stopped combing and reached for a printed flyer. "Our category," Kayo said, showing the flyer to Rosie, "is called Domestic House Cat, which includes every non-purebred cat there is. Homer and Diamond are domestic house cats. So is Webster. They have just as much chance of winning as any other house cat."

"Webster gets too excited around people he doesn't know. The last time we took him for a checkup, he bit the veterinarian."

"Cat show people know how to handle nervous cats," Kayo said. "If they didn't, they'd have shredded wrists."

Kayo read more of the flyer aloud: " 'All cats must be in decorated cages. Points will be given for unusual cage decoration.' "

"That would be fun," Rosie said.

"The cat show will be exciting and fun for the cats," Kayo said. "It can be an official Care Club project."

"We *have* been looking for a project," Rosie said, "and if Webster got used to his cage ahead of time, he might not get too nervous."

There was a knock at the door. Kayo looked through the peephole. "It's Sammy Hulenback," she whispered.

"Yuck. What does he want?"

"How should I know? Let's pretend we aren't here."

Sammy knocked again. "Kayo?" he called. "Open the door. I know you're in there. Rosie's bike and wagon are out here."

"We may as well see what he wants," Rosie said. "Otherwise he'll keep pestering us."

Kayo opened the door but did not invite Sammy inside.

"Do you want to see a dead squirrel?" Sammy said. "There's one in the street over by my house, squashed flatter than a piece of paper, with all its guts hanging out."

"Oh, gross," said Kayo.

"The poor little thing," said Rosie.

"Is that why you came?" Kayo said. "To tell us about a dead squirrel?"

"Sure. How many chances like this do you get? You'd better hurry because it won't be there long. My dad went to get a shovel so he could bury it."

"Well, it's nice to know that *someone* in your family has a heart," Kayo said.

"And a brain," added Rosie.

Sammy grabbed the cat show flyer out of Kayo's hand.

"Give me that," Kayo said.

"Cat show!" said Sammy. "Don't tell me you're planning to enter those scruffy strays of yours in a cat show!"

"They aren't scruffy," Kayo said.

"They sure won't win any prizes."

"Our cats have an excellent chance of winning first place," said Rosie.

"Ha!" cried Sammy. "So you *are* going to enter the cat show."

"May I please have my flyer back?" Kayo said.

"Maybe I'll come to the cat show, too," said Sammy as he read the rest of the flyer.

"They don't have a category for nerds," said Rosie.

Sammy handed the paper back to Kayo. "I

guess you don't want to see the squirrel, huh?"
he said.

"You have made some dumb errors before,"
Kayo said, "but you *really* struck out this time."
She slammed the door.

"I'll see you Saturday," yelled Sammy, "at the
cat show!"

"If Sammy comes to the cat show," Kayo said,
"he'll cause major league trouble. He's the most
rotten kid in the whole sixth grade. Make that
the whole school. No, make that the most rotten
kid in the universe."

"He likes you," Rosie said.

Kayo rolled her eyes in disgust. "I never met
such a twerp."

"He likes you," Rosie repeated. "He wants to
be your boyfriend. That's why he keeps coming
around all the time and trying to show off. He
wants you to like him back."

"If he thinks a dead squirrel will fill my heart
with romance, he is totally off base."

Rosie dropped to her knees and assumed a
deep, fake voice. "Kayo, my darling," she said,
"I brought you red roses, and chocolate-covered
cherries, and a squashed squirrel. Will you
marry me?"

Kayo did not laugh. "A dead squirrel is nothing to joke about at a Care Club meeting," she said.

"Sorry," said Rosie. She sat down and turned another page in the dictionary.

"We were discussing the cat show," Kayo said, "before Squirrel Brain interrupted us. It's at Clara Barton High School and there's a one-hundred-dollar prize in each category."

"One hundred dollars?" Rosie quit paging through the dictionary and gave Kayo her full attention. "In every category? Even the best domestic house cat will get one hundred dollars?"

"That's right," Kayo said. "I move that Care Club officially enter Webster, Homer, and Diamond in the Cat Fanciers Association Cat Show next Saturday." She waited for Rosie to second the motion.

"Sammy Hulenback could cause trouble," said Rosie.

"I do not plan to let Sammy Hulenback influence my vote," Kayo said.

"Neither do I," said Rosie. "I second the motion."

"All in favor of entering Homer, Diamond, and Webster in the cat show say *aye*."

"Aye," said Rosie.

"Aye," said Kayo.

"Those opposed?"

"Meow," said Homer.

"The motion is carried," said Kayo. "The cat show will be our first official Care Club project."

Kayo was glad to have something new to think about. If she and Rosie were busy making decorated cat cages, Kayo wouldn't have time to worry about the cat burglar's return.

Chapter 3

"If either of us wins," Kayo said, "let's split the prize. Fifty dollars each."

"If we win," Rosie said, "I don't think we should keep the prize money."

"What?" Kayo had already decided to use her fifty dollars to buy a new baseball glove. She even knew which glove she wanted. At that very moment it was displayed in the window of Big Five Sporting Goods Store, and Kayo rode her bike past daily, to be sure it was still there.

"Since the cat show is an official Care Club project," Rosie said, "we should use the money to help animals. The Care Club charter says we'll do whatever we can to help homeless animals, so if we win the prize, we should help some homeless animals."

"How are we going to do that?" said Kayo. "I don't know any homeless animals. If I did, I would adopt them and they wouldn't be homeless anymore."

"We can donate the prize money to The Humane Society," Rosie said. "They try to find homes for homeless animals."

Kayo hated to admit it, but she knew Rosie was right. She allowed herself to imagine the new glove on her hand one last time before she agreed to give away the prize money.

The next day Rosie's dad helped her build a cat cage, which she decorated like a tropical island. Red plastic hibiscus blossoms clung to the top and sides of the cage, and a fake orchid stood in the corner next to the sandy beach.

"It looks like a travel agency ad," Kayo said. "Where did you get the white sand? It's the same as the jar of beach sand that my uncle brought back from Hawaii."

"It's really cat litter," Rosie said. "The expensive kind."

"We always get what's on sale," Kayo said.

The Saunderses' phone rang. When Rosie answered, Sammy Hulenback said, "Be sure to read tonight's paper. It tells about Kayo getting robbed by the cat burglar."

"Oh," said Rosie, not sure whether to believe him or not.

"And tell Kayo I'll see her at the cat show tomorrow."

"We won't be there," Rosie said. "One of Kayo's cats is going to star in a movie, and we're leaving for Hollywood in the morning."

Rosie hung up. "That was Sammy," she said. "He said to tell you he'll see you at the cat show."

Rosie found the newspaper on the floor beside her dad's favorite chair. She read the headline out loud: LOCAL VICTIMS HOWL OVER CAT BURGLAR LOSSES. She and Kayo read the article together.

The cat burglar who has robbed numerous local homes in recent weeks struck three times yesterday at an apartment building on Yukon Drive. It is the first time the thief has robbed in daylight.

According to Police Chief Brian Stravinski, the triple burglary could be a sign that the cat burglar is getting overconfident and, therefore, more likely to take a risk that will result in his getting caught. So far, the elusive burglar has slipped in and out of fourteen homes. Losses have included cash, sterling silver flatware, watches, jewelry, numerous television sets, VCRs, computers, cameras, and other valuables.

The cat burglar is adept at covering his tracks; to date, there are no clues and no leads. Anyone with information about a possible suspect is urged to contact Chief Stravinski.

"Why do they call him a cat burglar?" Kayo said.

"Probably because he usually robs at night and cats like to be out at night. Or maybe it's because no one hears him, even when the victims are home, and cats can walk so quietly they aren't heard."

"Well, I think they should call the burglar something else," Kayo said. "It gives cats a bad name."

"Rat burglar," said Rosie as she put Webster in his new cage. "Rats are most active at night."

Rosie's dog, Bone Breath, sniffed around the cat cage, wagging his tail.

"For that matter," said Rosie, "why do they assume the burglar is a man? Maybe a woman robbed all those houses."

Cat Burglar on the Prowl

"Man or woman," Kayo said, "it gives me the creeps to know someone was in our apartment when we weren't home." To herself she added, What if he comes again?

She had told her mother what Sammy said about burglars who return, and Mrs. Benton had assured Kayo that it would not happen. "He didn't get that much of value from us," she said, "and thieves go where it's easy and fast to get in. If he came back to our apartment, he would have to shatter a window or force a door this time. Quit worrying."

Kayo tried to take her mother's advice, but it wasn't easy.

Webster rubbed the side of his face against the little beach umbrella that Rosie had fastened to the floor of the cage. He purred.

"He likes his cage," Rosie said, clearly relieved. "Maybe he won't bite the judge, after all."

Webster looked at the sandy beach. He started to scratch in it.

"Oh, no," said Rosie as Webster dug a hole in his beach and squatted over it. "He's using the beach for a litter box! What if he does that in front of the judges?"

"Be sure to take your pooper-scooper to the cat show," said Kayo.

By Saturday morning Kayo had turned her old

rabbit hutch into the perfect cage for Homer and Diamond: a miniature baseball stadium.

"Let's glue some of your baseball cards on the cage," Rosie suggested. "The good ones, like Ken Griffey, Junior."

Kayo put both hands on her head and looked as if Rosie had suggested she drink out of the toilet. "Are you kidding?" she cried. "It would wreck them if I put glue on the backs."

Kayo's long blond hair hung from beneath a Los Angeles Dodgers baseball cap. Her sweatshirt said, "Diamonds Are Forever" and showed a baseball field.

"You wouldn't have to glue them," Rosie said. "You could just stand them up inside the cage."

"If I had my best baseball cards in this cage, someone would try to steal them. I would never risk losing my baseball cards—not if the cat show prize was a zillion billion dollars. Never!" Kayo thumped her fist into her palm for emphasis. "Never, never, never!"

"Okay, okay. It was just an idea."

Mrs. Benton drove the girls to the Clara Barton High School gymnasium. As she drove, she turned on the car radio. A newscaster said, "There was another cat burglary in Oakwood last night. This time he took a computer and three hundred dollars while the family was asleep in the house."

Kayo shuddered.

The newscaster continued. "I'm with the victim right now. Please tell my listeners how it feels to wake up in the morning and realize a thief was in your house while you slept."

Mrs. Benton turned the radio off. "How does he think it feels?" she snapped. "What an idiotic question."

"It would be ineffable," said Rosie, taking out her notebook.

"What?" said Kayo.

"Don't tell me you've already forgotten what *ineffable* means," Rosie grumbled. "Sometimes I think you don't *care* about increasing your vocabulary."

Mrs. Benton stopped in front of the school and said she would pick the girls up at five o'clock. "Good luck," she said.

"Ineffable," said Rosie, "means beyond description. For example . . ."

Webster began yowling, drowning out further conversation.

Dozens of other people carried cats in cages, following the signs that said: CAT SHOW TODAY. Each contestant was assigned a number. Long rows of tables had numbers indicating where each cat's cage was supposed to go. Webster was number 32; Homer and Diamond were number 33.

The girls found their table and put the cages down on the proper numbers. Webster kept howling. He tried to squeeze underneath his bed and tipped it over.

There were sixty-eight entries in the Domestic House Cat division. One cage had a miniature desk, file cabinet, and toy computer. The cat's name was Software.

"We have some stiff competition," Rosie said.

Nearly two hundred cats filled the Purebred section. There were green velvet draperies around one cat's bed. Another cat had a silver water bowl with his name engraved on it. Rosie said, "I wonder if these people hire interior decorators to do their cages."

"Look at this one," Kayo said, pointing.

The cage was decorated in shades of purple. Dozens of purple rosettes hung overhead, each one proclaiming that this cat was Grand Champion or Best of Show or some other award. A framed needlepoint sign, stitched in purple and lavender yarn, said SAPPHIRE.

Kayo read the information on the sign that was attached to the table beside the purple cage. "Her full name is Sweet Sapphire the Sophisticat," she said. "She's a Chinchilla Persian."

The girls peered into Sapphire's cage. Sapphire had long white fur, flecked with silver on the tips. Her big emerald green eyes were rimmed with black, as if she had eyeliner on. Her fur was silky-looking, and she wore a jewel-studded purple collar.

"She *is* beautiful," Kayo said.

"She's no prettier than Webster," Rosie said. "She's no prettier than Homer and Diamond, either."

Kayo smiled. That was one thing she liked about Rosie; she was loyal.

Sweet Sapphire the Sophisticat had the first spot in the show, at the end of the table right beside the door.

Kayo finished reading the sign. "She's for sale," she said, and then gasped. "For nine hundred dollars."

"Nine hundred dollars for a cat," said Rosie, "is ineffable." She took out her notebook.

"Ineffable," said Kayo.

Rosie looked at her suspiciously. "Incapable of being described in words," she said.

"Oh, yes. I remember now."

"You will never build a large vocabulary if you don't use the words we learn," Rosie said.

Kayo swung an imaginary bat. "Professional baseball players don't need a large vocabulary."

"Yes, you do. Otherwise you'll sound stupid when you get interviewed on television."

It was almost time for the judging to begin when Rosie said, "Oh, no. Here comes Sammy Hulenback."

Chapter 4

"Did you have to bribe the officials to let you enter," said Sammy, "or is there a category for scuzziest cat?"

"Strike one," said Kayo.

"If you'll excuse us," said Rosie, "we're busy right now."

Sammy poked a finger at Homer and Diamond. "You should have combed them before you came," he said.

"Strike two," Kayo said. "Good-bye."

"I have to talk to Rosie," Sammy said. "Privately."

"Be my guest," said Kayo.

Sammy and Rosie walked away together. They talked for a minute, and then Rosie returned alone.

"Well?" said Kayo. "What did he want?"

"He wanted to know how he can get you to like him."

"He could move to Siberia."

"He was serious," Rosie said. "He really likes you."

"So what did you tell him?"

"I told him to write you a love poem."

"What? Are you crazy?"

"He'll never be able to do it. He always whines if we have to write a story in class. I figure he'll give up and find somebody else to like."

"What if he doesn't give up? The last thing I need is some drippy love poem from Sammy." Kayo removed her Los Angeles Dodgers baseball cap and wiped her brow, as if the very idea of a love poem from Sammy made her break out in a sweat.

"Shhh," said Rosie. "The judging is starting."

There were three judges in the Domestic House Cat competition, two women and a man.

Kayo's heart beat faster as the judges stepped up to Homer and Diamond's cage and peered at the scoreboard and dugouts Kayo had made. One judge read the names, Homer and Diamond, out loud and then told Kayo, "I'm a baseball fan, too." Kayo relaxed a little.

The woman judge opened the cage and reached

36

in. Homer behaved like an angel. He stood up, stretched, and walked into the judge's arms. He even purred. He let all three judges pet him, and when it was time to go back in the cage, he went right in, sat in his dugout, and began washing his whiskers, as if he was in a cat show every day of his life.

Diamond never got taken out. While the judges were petting Homer, Diamond discovered the Ping-Pong ball that Kayo had put in the cage. She had painted seams on it so it looked like a little baseball. Diamond swatted it with her paw, and the ball rolled across the pitcher's mound and into left field. Diamond batted it back across the pitcher's mound, toward home plate. She gave it another whack, and this time the ball rolled to the back of the cage and bounced off the wall.

"It's a triple," said one of the judges.

"No, it's an inside-the-park home run," said another.

Diamond picked up the ball in her teeth and put it in her dugout.

"What an original entry," said one judge.

Kayo leaned close to the cage and whispered, "Way to go, guys. That was an All Star effort."

When a judge opened Webster's cage, Webster hissed. The judged talked softly to him; Webster hissed again. His ears were so flat, it looked as if he didn't have any. He arched his back and his fur rose, making him look fluffier than he was.

Rosie crossed her fingers. *Please don't bite the judge,* she thought. *Please don't leave a bloody scratch on the judge's hand.*

"Let me try," said one of the other judges. This judge stuck his hand in the cage. Webster's paw flashed forward, claws out. Rosie closed her eyes. She wondered if cat show judges ever sued the cat's owner for having a vicious animal.

When she opened her eyes, the judge was holding a handkerchief on his wrist.

"Are you okay?" Rosie asked.

The judge nodded. "It happens all the time," he said.

The judges talked about the hibiscus blossoms, the palm tree, and the backdrop Rosie had painted of ocean waves and the setting sun. They seemed especially impressed by the fact that the sandy beach was Webster's cat litter. "Most entrants try to hide the litter," one judge said. "This one incorporates it into the setting in a natural way."

I can't believe it, thought Rosie. *I'm getting points for using cat litter.*

When the judges moved on, Rosie and Kayo sighed with relief.

"You are going to win First Place," Rosie said.

"Homer and Diamond were terrific for the judges."

"You have a chance, too," Kayo said. "The judges seemed really impressed with Webster's cage."

"Also his claws," said Rosie.

"What do you think The Humane Society will do with our one hundred dollars?"

"Maybe they'll buy cat food," said Rosie.

"Or pay to have some of the dogs bathed and groomed so they smell good when people come to look for a pet," said Kayo.

"I hope they do that," Rosie said. "When Bone Breath gets groomed, he comes home with a red ribbon behind one ear, and his breath smells like peppermint for almost a whole day."

By two-thirty the judging was completed.

The judges gave out ribbons in the Purebred section first. Sweet Sapphire the Sophisticat got a blue ribbon, which was no surprise to anyone.

Kayo and Rosie were still planning how The Humane Society should spend their donation, when the judges came to the Domestic House Cat section.

The judges walked slowly, as if they wanted to drag out the suspense. They turned down the aisle where Rosie and Kayo stood.

Rosie and Kayo crossed their fingers.

The judges placed a blue ribbon on the top of cage number 12. The excited owner shouted the good news to her mother on the other side of the room.

"Care Club won't be donating one hundred dollars," Rosie said. "Somebody else got first prize."

Someone else got second prize, too.

"We're getting shut out," Kayo said.

As the judges approached, Kayo and Rosie forced weak smiles. The judges placed a white ribbon on Homer and Diamond's cage. Kayo picked it up. It said THIRD in gold letters. She grinned. Third out of sixty-eight was not too bad. In fact, third out of sixty-eight was terrific.

"Congratulations," said all of the judges.

"Thank you," said Kayo. She held the ribbon so Rosie could read it. "Thank you very much!"

"You won!" cried Rosie. "You got a ribbon!" She stopped. The judges were in front of Webster's cage now. Instead of walking past, as Rosie expected, they handed her a gold-edged certificate.

"Congratulations," they said.

"Thank you."

Kayo and Rosie read the certificate together. " 'Best Cage Decoration: Domestic House Cat Division.' "

"I won, too!" Rosie cried. "We both won something!"

"We did it!" Kayo said. She felt the way she had when she became the first person in her school district to pitch a perfect baseball game. No hits; no walks; no errors. Seventeen strikeouts! Until now, that game had been the most exciting moment of her life, but this was even more fun because this time Rosie was a winner, too.

They raised their right hands and gave each other a high five. They laid the white ribbon on Homer and Diamond's cage and the certificate on Webster's cage, and they hugged each other and jumped in circles.

"We won!" they said over and over. "We both won a prize!"

When all the prizes had been distributed, one of the judges broadcast an announcement. "All the cats and owners who won ribbons or certificates will now participate in the Parade of Champions. Please line up as we call your number."

The judge's voice rose. "Leading the parade will be the overall Grand Champion cat, Saweeeet Saaapphire!" Everyone cheered as Sweet Sapphire's owner picked up her cage, with Sapphire in it, and carried her to the front of the parade.

All the third-place winners went next. Kayo picked up Homer and Diamond's cage and hurried to get in line. By the time the second- and first-place winners in each category were lined up, the line stretched clear back to the door.

At last they called for the winners of the Best Cage Decoration certificates to get in line. Domestic House Cat was the last category, which meant Rosie was the very last person in the parade.

The Parade of Champions was held in the second gymnasium. A large curtain divided the two gyms, but the announcer's voice could be heard clearly by those waiting in line.

Rosie had moved even with the cat show entry door, next to Sapphire's spot, when she heard the announcer say, "Third-place winner in the Domestic House Cat category is Kathryn Benton and her cats, Homer and Diamond."

Rosie wanted to watch. The cat show was an official Care Club event, and she wanted to see Kayo and Homer and Diamond as the crowd applauded. She wanted to cheer for them, not stand here in line.

Rosie set her cage on the number-one spot, beneath Sapphire's many purple rosettes, and hurried forward. She looked around the curtain into the second gym.

Homer and Diamond's cage was on a small table next to the announcer. Kayo stood beside it. All the spectators clapped and cheered as Kayo bowed.

Rosie put her fingers in her mouth and whistled shrilly through her teeth, the way she always did when Kayo hit a home run or struck out a batter.

Kayo heard the whistle, looked at Rosie, and waved.

Rosie waved back. This was great! This was absolutely the best thing she and Kayo had ever done.

Rosie watched until Kayo picked up her cage and marched to the side. She was glad to see there was a special place for the winners to sit with their cats and watch the rest of the parade. Kayo would get to see Rosie bow, too. It would be terrific to have Kayo cheer for her, for a change.

Smiling happily, she went back to get Webster and resume her place in line.

When she reached the number-one spot on the table, she stopped. All the purple ribbons still hung from the wire overhead; the sign telling that Sweet Sapphire was for sale for nine hundred dollars was still attached to the table; but the table space was empty.

Webster was gone.

Chapter

5

Rosie stared at the empty table.

Minutes earlier, when Rosie placed her cage on the table, Webster had been curled in a ball with his tail wound tightly around his feet. His silky black fur gleamed against the red and gold tropical print of his cat bed, and when Rosie said, "I'll be right back," Webster blinked his big yellow eyes and twitched his whiskers.

Now he was gone. Cage and all.

Rosie looked quickly around the gymnasium. She saw nothing unusual. The non-winning cats slept or meowed or licked their paws, just as they had all day.

The only people in the room stood in line for the Parade of Champions, each holding his own cat cage. No suspicious-looking person lurked about. No one was running away, carrying Webster in his cage. There was nothing to indicate that a beloved pet cat had just been stolen.

Not everyone, Rosie knew, was kind to animals. She had seen occasional television news accounts of abused creatures and was outraged by them. What kind of warped, horrible person would harm an innocent animal?

Now, as she realized that Webster was gone, she did not feel outrage; she felt fear—a cold, hard terror that started in the pit of her stomach and spread like ice water through her veins.

Who took Webster? Why? What did they plan to do with him?

Calm down, she told herself. There may be a simple reason why Webster isn't here. Probably someone realized his cage was in the wrong place, that's all, and they returned it to the proper table number.

Rosie rushed to space number 32, Webster's assigned place. Her eyes strained ahead of her feet, looking for the red hibiscus blossoms on the top of the cage. She knew even before she got to space 32 that Webster wasn't there.

Fighting back tears, Rosie ran toward the people who waited in the Parade of Champions line. They were close to where Webster had been when he was kidnapped. Maybe one of them saw what happened.

Ten minutes ago Rosie had thought the cat show was a wonderful project for Care Club. Now, as she raced toward the people in the parade line, it was no longer wonderful. It was horrible.

"Did anyone see someone take the cage from the end of that table?" she asked.

"That's the Grand Champion's spot," a man said. "She's in the other gym, at the head of the parade."

"I put my cat's cage there, just for a few minutes," Rosie said, "and now it's gone."

None of the others had seen anyone take Webster.

"I'll help you look for him, after the parade ends," someone said.

"Thanks," Rosie said, but she knew she could not wait that long.

Questions pounded through her head. Who took Webster? How will I get him back? What if the person who took him turns him loose? Webster, who had always been an indoor cat, would be terrified if he suddenly had to face traffic and barking dogs and all the other dangers of the streets.

Rosie's insides felt tied in knots, and the

cheese sandwich she had eaten earlier threatened to return to daylight.

Fighting panic, she hurried to the second gymnasium and went straight to the front, where the judges sat.

She tapped one of the judges on the shoulder and said, "Somebody stole my cat."

Startled, the judge looked at Rosie and said, "What?"

"My cat's gone. Somebody stole him."

"Aren't you the girl with the sandy beach, in the Domestic House Cat category?"

"Yes. My cat is Webster and he's gone." Rosie's voice got louder each time she said the terrible words.

"Shhh," said one of the other judges.

"I'll talk to you after the Parade of Champions ends," the first judge said.

"But . . ."

The judge motioned for Rosie to lean close while he whispered to her. "If someone was going to come in here and steal a cat," he said, "why would they take one of the house cats?"

Rosie felt tears forming. She didn't know why. All she knew was that Webster was gone and she had to get him back. She turned and ran out of the gymnasium.

As she went around the curtain, back to the

47

first gym, she heard footsteps running after her. Turning, she saw Kayo, holding Homer and Diamond's cage in her hands and her white ribbon in her teeth.

"Somebody stole Webster," Rosie said. By now her voice had an edge of hysteria. "I put him down so I could watch you take your bow, and when I went back, he wasn't there."

Kayo carried her cage back to spot number 33 and put it down. "Let's look outside," she said. "Maybe someone moved him, as a practical joke."

They went out the door next to Sweet Sapphire's number-one table space and walked along the sidewalk toward the parking lot.

"Look!" cried Kayo.

On the sidewalk in front of them lay a red plastic hibiscus blossom. "That came off Webster's cage," Rosie said. "Someone carried him this way."

"We'd better call your parents," Kayo said.

"I can't. Mom is interviewing a client for some important court case, and Dad was late for his deadline with next week's cartoons so he's down in his studio with the phone turned off. I'll get the upstairs answering machine."

"Then I'll call my mom."

They went to the phone at the front of the school, dialed, and waited while it rang ten times. "She isn't home," Kayo said.

Cat Burglar on the Prowl

"I'm calling the police," said Rosie. She punched 911, and when the emergency operator answered, Rosie said, "Someone stole my cat."

"This line is for emergency calls only," said the operator.

"This *is* an emergency. I had my cat at the cat show at Clara Barton High School and somebody took him. I found one of the flowers from his cage on the sidewalk. Tell the police to hurry. Use their sirens!"

"A missing cat is not an emergency," said the operator. "I suggest you put a Lost Cat ad in the newspaper."

"He isn't lost. He was kidnapped!"

"I cannot tie up an emergency phone line over a cat. Someone might need to call because they're having a heart attack or their house is on fire," the operator said, and she hung up.

Rosie started to cry. "Nobody believes me," she said.

"I believe you," Kayo said.

"They act like Webster isn't important."

"If nobody will help us," Kayo said, "we will help ourselves."

Rosie wiped her eyes and nose on her sleeve and took a deep breath. Kayo was right. It wouldn't help Webster to stand here sniffling.

The girls continued along the sidewalk to the parking lot.

"I had a terrible time attaching those hibiscus flowers to the cage," Rosie said, "and they were still loose. Maybe some more of them fell off and we can follow the thief's trail."

"Like Hansel and Gretel with the bread crumbs," Kayo said.

But they found no more flowers. Although they walked up and down the parking lot, there were few empty parking spaces; everyone was still inside, watching the Parade of Champions.

"It's only four o'clock," Kayo said. "My mom won't get here for another hour."

"Maybe the thief was on foot," Rosie said. "Maybe it was just kids doing something daring, and they've left the cage sitting under a tree somewhere."

"That would be pretty stupid," Kayo said, and then, seeing the look on Rosie's face, she added, "but kids do lots of stupid things."

"I'll bet it was Sammy Hulenback," Rosie said. "He acted jealous that we had our cats in a cat show, and it's exactly the sort of prank he would pull. He probably took Webster and hid him so he can pretend to find him and be a big hero."

"Of course!" said Kayo. "We should have thought of Sammy right away."

"Let's go to his house," Rosie said, "and catch him red-handed."

"I don't know where he lives. Do you?"

"We can look it up in the telephone directory."

They returned to the phone booth and looked in the directory. There was only one Hulenback.

"Maybe we should call first," Kayo said. "We can tell his parents what he did, and they can make sure Sammy doesn't do something senseless, like let Webster outside, before we get over there."

Rosie looked so horrified that Kayo quickly added, "I'll make the call," and stuck her quarter in the slot. "Hello," she said. "Is this Sammy Hulenback's house?" There was a pause and then Kayo said, "Oh. I see. Thank you very much." She hung up.

"What did they say?"

"It was Mr. Hulenback. He said Sammy went to the cat show," Kayo said.

"We *know* that."

"With his mother."

Kayo blinked. "Sammy's with his mother?"

"That's what his dad said. I thought we should look inside before we accuse him."

They hurried back into the school. The announcer was introducing the winner of the Best

Cage Decoration in the Purebred Division. The girls peered around the curtain at the audience sitting on the bleachers.

"There he is," said Kayo. "With his mother. I recognize her from when she brought Sammy's lunch to school a couple of times."

The announcer said, "Winner of Best Cage Decoration in the Domestic House Cat Division is Rosemary Saunders, with her cat, Webster."

There was a smattering of applause, which died away when Rosie did not appear. Everyone, including Sammy and his mother, looked around for Rosie.

"Will Rosemary Saunders please bring her cat forward?" asked the judge.

Fighting tears, Rosie ran out of the school and across the parking lot, with Kayo beside her. When they got to the street, they stopped.

"If Sammy didn't take Webster," Rosie said, "who did?"

Kayo had no answer.

Chapter

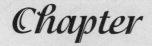

6

W̶e have to keep looking," Rosie said. "We can't just sit and wait for your mom to come while the thief gets farther and farther away."

"Should we split up or work as a team?" Kayo asked.

"We'd cover more ground separately," Rosie said, "but I think we should stay together. It's safer."

Kayo agreed. They decided to look six blocks in one direction and, if they didn't find any clues, return and go six blocks in a different direction.

Kayo—who ran two miles every day as part of her training to be a professional baseball player—took off like she was trying to steal a base; Rosie puffed after her. They passed a 7-Eleven store, an apartment building, and several houses. A small boy and girl were playing outside one of the houses.

Kayo stopped running and said, "Have you kids seen anyone carrying a cat cage?"

"We can't talk to strangers," said the girl.

"Someone stole our cat," Kayo said as Rosie caught up to her. "We're trying to find him."

"We aren't supposed to talk to strangers," said the little girl.

"Just answer yes or no," Rosie said. "Did anyone go past here with a black cat in a cage?"

"Yes," said the boy.

"I'm telling Mommy," said the girl.

"Was it a man or a woman?" Kayo asked.

The boy thought a moment. "A man," he said.

"What did he look like?" Rosie asked. She took the notebook and pencil out of her pocket.

The boy scowled, as if trying to remember. "He was big," he said, "and I think he had on jeans."

Rosie wrote down the description.

"What else?" Kayo said. "Tell us everything you can remember."

"I think he had on a blue jacket, but I'm not sure."

"Which way did he go?" asked Rosie.

The boy pointed in the direction Kayo and Rosie had come from. "That way."

Rosie and Kayo looked behind them. "Are you sure?" Kayo said.

The boy nodded. "I'm positive. I think there's a cat show at the school today because lots of people went that way carrying a cat in a cage."

Rosie stopped writing. "How long ago did you see the man carrying the black cat?" she asked.

The boy shrugged.

"Five minutes?" Kayo said. "Ten minutes?"

"Before lunch," the boy said.

Kayo groaned.

"You're going to get spanked," the little girl said, "when Mommy finds out you talked to strangers."

"They aren't strangers," the boy said. "They're girls."

"Thanks for your help," Rosie said. She and Kayo ran on.

"You're going the wrong way," the boy called. "The cats are at the school."

Six blocks later, having found no hibiscus blossoms or any other clue to suggest Webster might have been carried in that direction, the girls turned around and jogged back to the school.

As they passed the two children, the boy said, "I *told* you that was the wrong way. The man with the black cat went toward the school."

"Mommy's going to put you to bed without dinner," the little girl said.

Rosie and Kayo stopped at the school parking lot. Rosie sat down to catch her breath while Kayo went inside to be sure Homer and Diamond were all right.

"The man who owns Software agreed to keep an eye on Homer and Diamond while we're gone," Kayo said when she returned. "He said he had to stay until five o'clock anyway, and I said we'd be back by then."

"We went north first; now let's go east," Rosie said.

Kayo agreed.

The only thing Rosie found in the six blocks going east was the beginning of a blister on her left heel. She limped behind Kayo as they headed south.

They were almost ready to turn around, six blocks south of the school, when Kayo stopped running so abruptly that if Rosie had not been lagging behind, she would have bumped into her.

A blue van was parked at the curb, and for an instant, Rosie thought Kayo saw Webster in the van. Then she realized Kayo was pointing at the sidewalk.

"Sand," said Kayo. "Fine sand, as in good quality cat litter, as in sandy beach in Webster's cage."

Rosie knelt down and rubbed her fingers in the slight mound of sand. "It feels the same as what I used," she said.

Rosie looked around. A sudden chill of apprehension wriggled down the back of her neck. "This isn't exactly the best part of town," she whispered. She had been so busy trying to keep up with Kayo and looking down at the sidewalk for clues that she had not noticed when they left the tidy lawns behind and entered an area where empty beer cans and pieces of old newspaper littered the parched brown grass.

The sand lay on the sidewalk in front of a three-story apartment building that had once been painted white but was now a dingy gray. A weather-worn FOR RENT sign stuck in the yard looked almost as old as the building.

"I'll bet rats run here at night," Kayo said, "and spiders build nests in the corners of the rooms."

Rosie gulped. Rats and spiders were not high on her list of favorite things. She walked to the curb and looked inside the van. "There's sand on the seat," she said.

"We shouldn't jump to conclusions," Kayo said. "Maybe the person who owns the van just came home from the beach."

"Maybe."

"Or maybe," Kayo said, "this van was used to drive Webster here from the cat show."

Rosie's stomach lurched. She looked again at the run-down old apartment building. "Maybe Webster is hidden in this building," she said. Memories of Webster sped through her mind, like a slide show on fast-forward. She saw baby Webster, a tiny black fluff ball with legs, so small he fit in Rosie's palm. She saw Webster curled on Rosie's bed, purring, and Webster rolling on the kitchen floor, playing with his catnip mouse. She saw Webster sitting on the windowsill, making low meowing sounds as he watched the birds outside, and Webster waiting beside his food bowl for Rosie to give him dinner. A tear trickled down Rosie's cheek.

"Let's go around in back," Kayo said.

This time Rosie led the way. She tiptoed, even though there was no sign of anyone in or out of the building. Kayo followed her across the brittle brown grass and along the side of the building. A driveway, its concrete buckled from tree roots, led to an old garage at the back of the property. Twice the girls stopped to glance behind them. The whole neighborhood seemed deserted.

The backyard looked even worse than the front. Two battered cars were parked near the garage, and some rusty lawn furniture lay tipped over, with knee-high thistles growing through the rungs of the chairs.

"The people who live here shouldn't want a pet like Webster," Kayo said nervously. "He'd have burrs in his fur all the time."

"Whoever took him," Rosie said, "didn't do it because they want a pet. I don't think it was kids playing a trick, either. When Webster was stolen, his cage was in Sweet Sapphire's place on the table. I think the thief wanted Sweet Sapphire and got Webster by mistake."

"That might be a plus," Kayo said. "If the thief thinks Webster is worth nine hundred dollars, he'll take good care of him."

They headed back to the front of the apartment building. As they rounded the corner of the building, Kayo said, "Look."

Rosie looked.

A red hibiscus blossom lay half-hidden in the weeds beside the front steps.

Chapter

7

*R*osie picked up the flower and turned it over in her hand. "It's one of mine," she whispered. "It still has the twistie on it that I used to fasten the flowers to the cage."

Kayo whispered, too: "What do we do now?"

Rosie did not answer. She stuffed the plastic flower in the pocket of her jeans and climbed the steps of the building.

Kayo hesitated. "Maybe we should go back to the school and wait until my mom comes and have her come back here with us," she said.

"By then," Rosie said, "it might be too late. We don't know what the thief plans to do with Webster. What if he has already sold him? What if he puts him on a plane to Alaska? What if he discovers he *isn't* worth nine hundred dollars so he decides to get rid of him?" Rosie, who was never at a loss for words in the best of circumstances, rattled nervously on about every possibility, all of them bad.

Kayo took the Dodgers cap off her head, turned it around, and jammed it on backward, the way she always did when she had runners on base and needed to throw the best pitch she had. Then she climbed the steps and stood beside Rosie.

Together, they pushed open the door and stepped inside.

The hallway smelled musty, and the worn carpet had not seen a vacuum cleaner in recent history. The dim lightbulb which dangled down revealed that there were three apartments on the first level, with a stairway leading up to a second floor. A second door at the far end of the hall led to the backyard.

Rosie swallowed hard. Then she stepped up to the first door and knocked. Kayo stayed behind with one hand on the outside doorknob, ready to open it and bolt, if necessary. No one answered.

"Your turn," Rosie whispered.

Kayo reluctantly removed her hand from the doorknob and walked to the second door. This one had a small brass nameplate that said MRS. HELEN WATSON. Kayo tapped lightly.

"Harder," said Rosie.

Kayo pounded.

The door cracked open an inch. A small white-haired woman peered out.

"Mrs. Watson?" said Kayo.

The woman did not answer.

"Excuse me, Mrs. Watson," said Kayo. "We're looking for our cat, and I wonder if you might have seen it."

"Come again, dearie?" said Mrs. Watson.

"Our cat is missing," Rosie said, "and we think he's somewhere in this building."

"What's that, you say?"

"A cat!" Kayo shouted. "Have you seen a cat?"

"Your hat? What kind of hat is it?"

"Not hat. Cat," Rosie said.

"Cat," said Kayo. "Meow. Meow."

Mrs. Watson smiled and opened the door a bit more. "Oh!" she said. "Your cat!"

"Yes. My cat is missing," Rosie said and then repeated, more loudly, "Missing. Cat."

Mrs. Watson raised her eyebrows. "Why would someone be kissing your cat? Wouldn't they get fur in their mouth?"

"Not kissing," said Rosie. *"Missing.* Someone took him. *They took my cat!"*

Mrs. Watson scowled and put her hands on her hips. "Who shook him? Poor little cat."

Rosie and Kayo glanced at each other. "Thanks for your help," Rosie said. "We have to go now."

"Yes," said Kayo. "It was nice talking to you."

"I hope you find your hat," said Mrs. Watson.

No one answered their knock at the third door, so they climbed the stairs to the second floor.

The floor plan of the second floor was exactly like the first floor—three apartments. Three times, they knocked on doors. Three times, nobody answered.

"Everybody's at work," Kayo said.

"It's Saturday. Someone should be home on Saturday."

"Maybe the apartments are empty." Kayo held her nose. "The way this place smells, it would be pretty hard to find tenants."

They climbed the stairs to the third and last floor. Rosie knocked on the first door. No answer.

As they approached the second door, they heard angry voices coming from inside the last apartment at the end of the hall. Rosie put her finger to her lips. Kayo nodded. Quietly they went closer, listening intently.

"You fool!" a woman shouted. "This is the stupidest trick you've pulled yet."

"Stupid?" said a man. "Stupid! It's worth nine hundred dollars, so what's stupid about that? It's twice what I got from that house on Riverview Drive that *you* picked out."

"What makes you think it's worth nine hundred dollars?" the woman said.

"Because it's a grand champion, that's why."

"That," said the woman, "is no grand champion cat. It isn't even a purebred."

Rosie reached for Kayo's hand. Their fingers intertwined as they stood in the dim hallway, straining to hear more.

"It is, I tell you," said the man. "This cage was sitting in the middle of fifty purple ribbons. There were signs hanging all around it: grand champion this, grand champion that. Best of Show. Best of Breed. Best of Everything in the World. And it's for sale, for nine hundred dollars."

Rosie felt perspiration on her upper lip. She should never have set Webster's cage in Sweet Sapphire's spot, even for a moment. She dropped Kayo's hand and inched closer to the door. Kayo followed.

"I don't care if there were neon billboards," the woman snapped. "Any moron can see that this is a plain old alley cat, and it is not worth a dime."

Rosie glared at the door. Kayo clenched her right fist and punched it into her left palm, the way she did when she had her baseball glove on.

The woman continued, "You were supposed to see if Arnold's Pawnshop is open yet so we can get rid of some of this stuff."

"I went to Arnold's. He's still closed. I asked about him in the doughnut shop next door, and they said he went on a cruise through the Panama Canal."

"Using the money he makes on what *we* bring him," the woman grumbled.

"I just happened to pass the cat show on my way home," the man said.

"Just happened to pass it, my foot. Ever since you tried to take a cat from that apartment on Yukon Drive and couldn't catch it, you've had cat on the brain."

Rosie stopped glaring. Kayo stopped punching. They looked at each other. The hair on the back of Kayo's neck prickled in alarm. *She* lived on Yukon Drive.

The woman's voice dropped, and the girls leaned closer to the door, pressing their ears against it in order to hear.

"I told you not to steal the grand champion cat," the woman said. "I told you it would be more bother than it was worth. But did you listen to me? Oh, no. Not only did you not listen, but you were too stupid to take the real grand champion; you got an impostor."

"I'm not staying here while you insult me, Babs," the man said. "If you don't like the way I operate, you can find yourself a new partner."

The door flew open.

Rosie and Kayo tumbled into the room, landing in a tangle of arms and legs on the floor.

Chapter

8

For an instant, nobody moved.

Rosie and Kayo lay on the floor, stunned at being discovered. The man towered over them, his hand still on the doorknob.

The woman stood across the room, staring at them with a shocked expression. "What do you think you're doing?" she demanded.

Kayo scrambled to her feet. She reached down to help Rosie up. As soon as Rosie was on her feet, Kayo cried, "Run!" and sprinted past the flabbergasted man, with Rosie right behind her.

The man reached for Rosie as she went past. His hand clutched her shirtsleeve, but Rosie kept moving. There was a ripping sound as the seam of her sleeve tore. The sleeve slipped out of the man's fingers, and Rosie dashed after Kayo.

"Don't let them get away," the woman yelled.

Kayo and Rosie galloped down the stairs.

Footsteps thundered behind them.

Kayo and Rosie passed the second-floor landing and started down the stairs toward the street below. Behind them the woman shouted, "Faster, Ed!"

Just as they got to the bottom of the stairs, the man lunged at Rosie, grabbing her shoulder from behind.

Rosie screamed.

Kayo stopped running and turned to look. That small hesitation allowed the man to grab her with his other hand.

He was a big man, with thick shoulders and strong hands.

Rosie kicked the man in the leg. He cursed but did not let go.

Kayo twisted and fought, trying to free herself from his grasp, but his fingers were like a vise, and the more she struggled, the tighter he held her.

The woman reached the bottom of the stairs and grabbed Rosie's other arm, twisting it behind her until Rosie cried out.

"Go back up the stairs," the woman said. "Now."

The woman stayed behind Rosie, still holding Rosie's arm behind her, as Rosie started slowly back up the stairs. The man, having let go of Rosie, used both hands on Kayo, shoving her up the stairs, too.

When they reached the apartment, the couple pushed Kayo and Rosie inside and immediately shut the door. The man stood in front of the closed door, blocking any attempt at escape.

For the first time Rosie and Kayo glanced around the room. It looked more like a warehouse than somebody's home. There was no couch, no chairs, no furniture of any kind. Instead, there were computers, television sets, stereo systems, and tape players. There were also a dozen bulging pillowcases. Webster's cage rested on top of a large TV.

Rosie rushed to Webster's cage and looked inside. "He's okay," she told Kayo. "We're here," she told Webster. "Don't be scared."

"Oh, great!" the woman said. "Not only did you take the wrong cat, you let a couple of kids see you do it."

"Nobody saw me do it."

"No? I suppose these girls just happened to drop in for a cup of tea."

"I want my cat back," Rosie said.

"*Your* cat?" the man said. "A kid owns the Grand Champion cat, worth nine hundred dollars?"

"I own Webster."

"Who isn't worth a nickel," said Kayo, coming to stand beside Rosie. Before Rosie could protest, she added, "So you may as well give him back to us."

"That's right," Rosie said. "We'll just take him home, since he's no good to you."

"You," said the woman, "are going nowhere."

Kayo looked quickly around the room. There was no telephone. Nobody knew where she and Rosie were, and there was no way to call for help.

"We're going to have to move out," the woman said. "Start loading the van."

"Now?" the man said. "In daylight?"

"*I'm* not the one who said we could sell kittens for nine hundred bucks apiece," the woman said, "and *I'm* not the one who let two junior detectives follow him home." She pointed a finger at him, the long red nail aimed at his chest. "*You're* the one who thought it would be funny for a cat burglar to steal a cat," she said. "Not me."

Kayo turned pale. She reached for Rosie, to steady herself. It was him, the cat burglar! This mean-looking man had walked through her home. This man had stolen her belongings. He had even tried to steal Homer or Diamond. No wonder they acted so spooked that day and hid under the bed.

She glanced quickly around the room, but she did not see Great-grandmother Kearney's silver tea set. He must have sold it already. Waves of anger washed over Kayo; she clenched her teeth together as she watched the man.

"You had to have your little joke, didn't you?" the woman continued. "Won't it be a riot, you said, for the cat burglar to steal a cat? Ha, ha, ha. Well, stop laughing and start moving, because it won't be funny if the cops come looking for these kids."

It's worse, Kayo decided, to know what he looks like.

It was awful before, when he was a vague form without features in Kayo's imagination, but it was even more horrible to see the man's dark, angry eyes and his square, wide jaw and to know he was the one who entered her home uninvited and robbed her.

The man glared at Rosie and Kayo. "What are we going to do with them?" he said.

"I'll worry about them; you just start moving this stuff out of here. We'll take it to Clarence."

"Clarence won't give us half what it's worth,"

the man grumbled. "I say we wait for Arnold to get back."

"Half is better than nothing, which is what we'll have if the cops come snooping around looking for these kids."

"Clarence is a crook and a cheat," the man said, but even as he complained, he picked up a TV and carried it toward the door.

"You girls are going to stay here," the woman said. "And don't bother yelling for help. The only other person in this building is old Mrs. Watson, who's deaf as a dead man."

The woman picked up two stereos and followed the man, closing the door behind her. The key clicked in the lock.

"What are we going to do?" Rosie said. "We're standing in a room full of stolen merchandise." She tried the door, to be sure it was locked. It was.

"Maybe she was lying about nobody being home. We didn't knock at the other apartment on this floor, the closest one. Let's yell."

"Help!" screamed Rosie.

"Help! Help!" yelled Kayo.

They banged their fists on the wall between the two apartments. "Help!" they shouted.

There was no response.

"Maybe someone in a different building will

hear us," Rosie said. She ran to the window and tried to open it, but years of paint had hardened around the wooden window ledge and the window did not budge.

Kayo stood beside her, and they both shoved at the same time. The window stayed firmly closed.

Kayo picked up a portable stereo. "Stand back," she said. Holding the stereo in front of her stomach, she rammed it into the window, shattering the glass. Pieces of glass fell to the backyard below, and a sprinkling of glass showered to the floor. A few jagged shards remained attached to the windowframe. Still using the stereo, Kayo broke them loose, so they tumbled out and down.

"Help!" yelled Rosie, through the empty window.

"Help!" screamed Kayo.

A voice below called, "You're wasting your breath."

The girls quit shouting and leaned out the window. To their left, the blue van was now parked close to the back of the house, on the driveway where Rosie and Kayo had walked earlier. They saw the man fold down the van's backseats and put the TV inside.

"They're the only ones who hear us," Kayo said.

The man put the stereos inside the van and removed a wheeled dolly, the kind Rosie's dad rented when they moved their refrigerator. He pulled the dolly along the back of the apartment building, kicking aside the glass from the broken window, and up the back steps. The woman followed.

"Here they come," Kayo said.

"What do you think they'll do with us?" Rosie said. She stood next to Webster's cage, with her fingers poked through the wire next to Webster's head.

"They'll probably take all this stuff out and leave us locked up in here. I wish we had told someone where we were going. They won't have any clue where to look for us."

"It could be days before we're found," Rosie said.

"Weeks," Kayo said. "How long can a person live without food or water?"

"What if they take us with them?" Rosie said. Her heart pounded even faster than it had when she was a finalist in the fifth-grade spelling bee and got the word plagiarism.

Kayo stared at her. "You mean, kidnap us?"

"If they leave us here, they know we'll be found eventually and we can identify them. What if they . . ." She hesitated, hating to put her thought into words because that would make it seem more real.

74

"What?" said Kayo. "What are you thinking?"

Rosie blurted it out. "What if they take us somewhere and get rid of us?"

"They didn't have a gun, did they?" Kayo asked.

"We didn't see a gun. That doesn't mean they don't have one."

"Oh."

"And there are other ways to get rid of us besides shooting." Rosie's voice dropped to a whisper. "Knives," she said. "Hanging. Drowning. Strangulation."

"Stop it!" Kayo cried.

Chapter

The key clicked. The door opened.

"I told you it wouldn't do any good to yell," the woman said. "No one heard you except us, and no one will."

"My mother is an attorney," Rosie said.

"Oh, great!" said the woman. "Did you hear that, Ed? Not only did you let two kids follow you home and catch us with all the evidence, one of them is the daughter of a lawyer. That's all we need, an outraged mama demanding justice in court."

The man rolled the dolly into the room and began stacking it with stereos and computers.

"If you let us go right now without hurting

us," Rosie said, "she would not press any charges against you."

"Do you think I'm a fool?" the woman said. "If we let you go right now, you'd be on your way to the cops before we could back out of the driveway."

"On the other hand," Kayo said, "if you *don't* let us go right now, Rosie's mom will throw the book at you in court."

"You don't scare us, missy," the man said. "Mama can only prosecute people she can find. And she won't be finding us."

"Maybe we shouldn't leave them here," the woman said. "The neighborhood around the cat show is the first place that will get searched."

"I'm not taking them with us. No way."

"Not permanently. Just far enough away that it won't be so easy to find them."

"You heard them screaming for help. Loud as lions. How are you going to keep two pair of lungs like that quiet in the van?"

"There are ways," the woman said.

The man laughed.

Rosie gulped and looked at Kayo.

The man pushed the full handcart toward the door. The woman picked up one of the bulging pillowcases and followed him out of the room. Once more, they locked the door behind them.

"What creeps," muttered Kayo. She paced around the room, socking her right fist into her left palm over and over, as she tried to think how to escape.

Webster let out a mournful yowl. "I'm sorry," Kayo said as she put her fingers through the chicken wire and stroked the cat's head. "I didn't think the cat show would end like this."

Rosie removed the notebook and pencil from her pocket and began writing.

"Let's hide notes inside the VCRs," she said. "Whoever finds them will call the police, and they'll know where to look for us."

Kayo looked to see what Rosie was writing. The note said, "Help. Call police. Rosie Saunders and Kayo Benton are locked in an old apartment . . ." Rosie stopped writing. "We don't know the address," she said.

"Just say six blocks south of Clara Barton High School, on the dead-end street."

"Right." Rosie finished the note and handed it to Kayo, who folded it in quarters and stuck it inside one of the stolen VCRs, in the slot where a video tape would be inserted.

While Kayo did that, Rosie wrote an identical second note. There were three VCRs; the girls put notes in all three of them.

They looked out the window. The man and the woman were still loading the van.

"We could drop something on him," Kayo said. "They walk directly under this window when they go between the back door and the van. We could drop a TV or a stereo out the window and hit him on the head and knock him out. Then it would be two of us against one of her."

"What if we miss? Or what if it hits him but doesn't knock him out? He would be furious."

"I have good aim," Kayo said. "Better yet, let's each drop something. If we hit both of them, there's a good chance at least one would not be able to come after us." She picked up a small portable television set. "By the time this drops two stories and hits him on the head, it will do plenty of damage," she said.

Rosie picked up a stereo speaker. "I'll aim for her; you aim for him," she said.

They carried the TV and the speaker to the window.

"The window isn't wide enough," Rosie said. "We can't do it at the same time."

"I'll go first," Kayo said. "When the TV hits him and he falls down, she'll go over to see how badly he's hurt, and then you can bop her with the stereo speaker."

"Right."

Kayo looked out the window, waiting for the man to leave the van and walk toward the back door. She knew she would have to release the television a second or two before he was below the window, to allow time for it to drop. She tried to calculate where he should be when she let go.

"What if you kill him?" Rosie said.

Kayo put her head back inside and turned to Rosie. "Do you think it might?" Much as she wanted to get away from the cat burglar and the cat woman, Kayo had no desire to be a murderer.

"These things are pretty heavy and it's a long way down."

"I don't want to kill anyone," Kayo said. "Not even someone as rotten as the cat burglar."

"On the other hand," Rosie said, "they might kill us if we don't do this."

Gripping the television set, Kayo turned back to the window.

Rosie peered over her shoulder. "Here he comes," she whispered.

Kayo breathed faster. She put the TV set through the open window, resting her arms on the window ledge, and leaned out, watching the man, hoping he would not look up.

His eyes were down as he steered the dolly

toward the back steps. The woman was rearranging something in the van.

When he gets to the second old lawn chair, Kayo thought, I'll let go. *Just three more steps.*

She licked her dry lips.

Two more steps. Get ready.

She lifted her arms off the window ledge and held the television set suspended in the air.

Now!

Chapter

10

Kayo pulled the TV back through the window and set it on the floor. Her hands shook and she felt short of breath, as if she had been running. "I can't do it," she said. "Not when it could kill him."

"Whew." Rosie let her breath out in relief and patted Kayo's shoulder. "I didn't really want you to," she said. "No matter what bad things he has done, it would be wrong for us to kill him."

For a moment silence filled the room as each girl tried to think what to do next. Then Kayo said, "We broke the wrong window. Let's break the one that faces the street. That way we can yell for help if anyone goes past." She hurried across the room to the high narrow window that faced the front side of the building. She looked out. "Oh, my," she said softly.

Rosie ran over and looked out, too. Straight below the window, about eight feet down, was a roof. The apartment underneath them apparently had more rooms than the one they were in; one of the rooms jutted out toward the street.

"We can jump to that roof," Kayo said.

"But we'd still be two stories up. We can't jump from there to the street."

Kayo pointed to a tree whose branches stretched over the far end of the roof below them. "We'll jump to the roof and climb down the tree," she said. Without waiting for a response, she grabbed the portable stereo again and smashed the second window. Rosie used the stereo speaker to push out the jagged pieces of glass around the window's edge.

"I'll go first," Kayo said. She climbed on to the window ledge, turned so she faced the room, and then squatted, putting her hands next to her shoes. Holding tight to the ledge, she extended her feet down the outside of the building.

She dangled there for a split second and then let go. She dropped easily to the roof, but instead of landing on her feet, she lost her balance and sat down hard in the middle of the broken glass.

Rosie climbed onto the window ledge and turned so her back faced the outside, just as Kayo had done. She squatted and put one leg at a time carefully out the window. She hung there, with her feet swinging freely next to the side of the building.

"Wait a second before you drop down," Kayo said. "I'll try to steady you when you land so you don't fall in the glass."

"Hurry," Rosie said. "I think I hear them opening the door." She clung to the window ledge while Kayo stood up.

"Okay," Kayo said. "Let go."

Her words were covered by a louder, deeper voice directly over Rosie's head. "Here they are! They've gone out the window!" At the sound of the man's voice, Rosie opened her hands.

She wasn't fast enough. At the instant her fingers released the window ledge, his hands grasped her wrists.

"Run for help!" Rosie shouted.

Looking up, Kayo saw the cat burglar yank Rosie upward and back through the window.

Kayo rushed toward the tree.

"Hurry!" yelled Rosie.

Kayo stopped at the edge of the roof. It wasn't going to be as easy to get into the tree as it had looked from above. The branches that touched the roof were too small to hold her weight. She would have to jump down and out, toward the center of the tree—and what if she missed? She peered over the edge of the roof; it was a long way down.

She looked up at the window. Rosie was out of sight, and the cat burglar was climbing out. If I'm going to jump into the tree, she thought, I have to do it now. Her eyes darted across the branches, looking for one that was both sturdy enough to hold her and close enough to jump to. There were none.

She kneeled on the edge of the roof and looked over, wondering which would be worse—to jump off and be injured or to have the cat burglar capture her again.

Thud! The whole roof shook as the cat burglar landed behind Kayo.

A string of expletives exploded like firecrackers. Looking over her shoulder, Kayo saw that the man had slipped when he landed and, putting out a hand to catch himself, had cut his palm on the broken glass.

She looked at the ground once more, knowing in her heart it would be foolish to jump. The chances for permanent injury, or even death, were too great. Better to stay here with Rosie and face their attackers together than to kill herself leaping off a roof, leaving Rosie to deal with the crooks alone.

She stood and turned to face the cat burglar. He had his cut hand in his mouth. She watched him spit blood on the roof.

Loud rock music came out of nowhere. For an instant Kayo thought the woman inside had turned on one of the CD players or a television set. Then she realized the music came from behind her. Whirling around, she saw a car coming down the street, its radio blaring.

"Help!" Kayo shouted. She waved both arms over her head and yelled at the driver. "Stop! Stop!"

The cat burglar covered the distance between them in two large strides, quickly clamping one hand over Kayo's mouth and pinning her arms to her sides with the other hand.

"Mmmmph!" said Kayo. She saw the driver of the car zoom by without looking her way; his wrists rested on the steering wheel, his fingers snapped in time to the music.

As the car drove out of sight, Kayo felt like a rag doll with no stuffing. All she wanted to do was crumple in a heap and cry.

The man had other ideas.

"You little monster," he said. "If you want to get down so bad, maybe I should help you do it." He shoved Kayo toward the edge of the roof.

"Stop that, Ed!" The woman yelled out the window, but the man paid no attention.

Kayo squirmed and kicked at the man, trying to get away. He gave her another push toward the edge.

"Use your head for a change," the woman said. "If you push her off that roof and she lives, she'll go for help and she can identify us."

The man stopped pushing Kayo toward the edge of the roof. He put his hands on her shoulders and turned her around so she faced him. He glared at her for a second before he shoved her back underneath the broken window, where the woman was watching.

He bent over. "Get on my shoulders," he ordered.

Kayo did as she was told. When the man stood up, Kayo easily reached the window ledge and climbed back inside.

"The tree was farther away than it looked," Kayo told Rosie. "I was afraid I would fall if I jumped."

"We should stick together anyway," Rosie said. "I'm glad you're still here with me."

From outside the man yelled, "How am I supposed to get back in? I need something to stand on."

The woman picked up the portable TV that

Kayo almost threw on the man's head, carried it across the room, and dropped it out the other window onto the roof. By standing on it, the man was able to reach up, grasp the window ledge, and hoist himself back inside.

As soon as he was back in the room, he stomped toward Rosie and Kayo. "Let me at them," he growled.

Rosie and Kayo backed away.

"Forget it, Ed," the woman said. "You're not touching those girls."

"You want to bet? They tried to outsmart us. They almost succeeded! If the kid in that car had not had his music blasting, the cops would be on their way over here right now." He licked the cut on his hand again. "Well, nobody messes with Ed Maloon and gets away with it. I always get revenge."

"That may be so," the woman replied, "but right now, it's more important to get the rest of this stuff out of here before the cops show up than it is for you to get even with a couple of kids."

"It won't take me five minutes to teach these two a lesson they won't forget." The man raised his fist. "And I'm going to enjoy every second of these five minutes."

Chapter

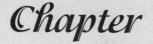

11

*T*he woman put her hand on the man's arm, restraining him. "You can have your five minutes of revenge after we get everything delivered to Clarence," she said. "Not before."

The man hesitated, glaring at the girls.

"You heard me, Ed," the woman said.

He lowered his arm and walked away from them. "If I have to wait," he said, "I'll take ten minutes."

He loaded the dolly, piling on all but two of the remaining computers. Before he left, he said, "Go in the bathroom and take a good look at your pretty little faces. They won't look that way much longer."

The woman lingered after he was gone. "Jumping out the window was not a smart idea," she said. "If you try to pull anything else, I guarantee you I won't keep Ed away from you next time. Do you understand?"

Rosie and Kayo nodded.

"All right, then."

After the woman left, Kayo said, "I'm sorry, Rosie. I shouldn't have suggested that we jump out the window and climb down the tree. It didn't work, and now he's mad at you because of my dumb idea."

"It wasn't a dumb idea," Rosie said. "It might have worked. Besides, I'm the one who got us into this in the first place by putting Webster in the wrong place at the cat show."

"Let's not waste time on what can't be changed," Kayo said. "There has to be a way to get out of this mess." She paced around the apartment, trying to think. As she entered the bathroom, she stubbed her toe on a piece of loose linoleum.

"Rosie," she said. "Look at this."

When Rosie got to the bathroom, Kayo was on her hands and knees, pulling pieces of linoleum away from the base of the toilet. A dank, moldy smell filled the small bathroom.

"This floor is full of rot," Rosie said. "Maybe we can make a hole big enough to drop through.

We could get out the door of the apartment below and go to Mrs. Watson's apartment and call the police."

Rosie wrinkled her nose. "Yuck," she said. "It stinks under this old floor." Stinky or not, she grabbed an edge of the linoleum and yanked a piece off. Below the linoleum was another layer of flooring, even more rotten and smelly than the first. The girls tugged that off, too, throwing the torn pieces into the bathtub.

After tearing off three layers of floor—one brown, one yellow, and one green—in a two-foot circle, they finally got down to plywood. The wood was damp and clearly rotten, but when Kayo tried to loosen the wood with her fingers, all she managed to do was get a splinter in her thumb and break a fingernail.

Rosie poked and dug at it, too, but the plywood remained firmly in place.

"We need a pry bar," Rosie said, "or at least a screwdriver."

"How about a knife?" Kayo asked.

"Where are we going to get a knife?"

"The newspaper said the cat burglar stole silverware. There might be a knife in one of those pillowcases."

Rosie stood up. "You're a genius," she said. "Maybe they even stole some tools. Burglars like tools, don't they, to help them break into safes? If we can find a hammer, we can forget about digging a hole in the floor. We'll pound the metal hinge pins loose and take the hinges off the door and escape."

Wiping their filthy hands on their jeans, Kayo and Rosie hurried back to the main room. Rosie sat on the floor and looked in one of the bulging pillowcases. "Wow!" she said. "Look at this."

Kayo peered into the pillowcase. It was filled with gold jewelry, watches, ten- and twenty-dollar bills, coins, and clocks—all jumbled together as if they had been thrown quickly into the pillowcase and never sorted out. She wondered if one of the clocks belonged to her mother. She wasn't sure she would recognize it, if it was there.

Rosie started digging through the goods in the pillowcase. "Maybe they stole a cellular telephone," she said. "We could call for help right now, before they come back upstairs."

Kayo opened a pillowcase, too, and began pawing through it. When she found a pile of one-dollar bills, rubber-banded together, she removed six of them and stuffed the bills into the pocket of her jeans. She knew money wouldn't help them escape, but it made her feel better to have her mother's six dollars back.

Rosie opened a second pillowcase and searched quickly through the contents. "Same kind of stuff," she said. "He must grab it from dresser tops and out of drawers and just throw it all in a pillowcase."

"Oh!" Kayo said. "Oh, my gosh."

Rosie looked to see what Kayo had found. Kayo had her hand in one of the pillowcases. She withdrew it slowly, looking as if she had discovered a queen's priceless golden crown.

"What is it?" said Rosie. "Did you find a hammer? Or a screwdriver?"

Kayo turned to Rosie and held out her arm, cradling a baseball in the palm of her hand. She rolled it over in her hand, examining it.

"Mickey Mantle," she said, her voice tinged with awe. "This ball is signed by Mickey Mantle."

"No kidding," said Rosie. "It must be valuable." She turned her attention back to the contents of the pillowcases.

"Valuable!" Kayo said. "I'd give a year's allowance for this ball. I wonder who it belongs to."

"They're coming," Rosie said as she heard voices outside the door. "Quick. Put it back. We don't want them to know we've been snooping."

But Kayo did not put it back. She tipped up her Dodgers cap, shoved the baseball underneath it, and put the hat back down, twisting it so it faced forward again. She stood straight as a flagpole, keeping her neck stiff so the ball wouldn't roll off her head.

"You can't take that baseball," Rosie whispered. "It doesn't belong to you."

"It doesn't belong to them, either. I'll turn it in to the police so they can give it back to its owner."

The key clicked in the lock.

"Oh," said Rosie. "I thought you were going to steal it."

"I can't steal it. It's already stolen."

The door opened. The man pushed the dolly into the room, glaring at the girls as he did. He and the woman were still arguing about whether to leave the girls in the empty room or take them along.

"They'll slow us down too much," the man said. "And Clarence will see them and ask questions. It would be just like him to call in an anonymous tip to the cops the minute we leave his place."

"We could tie them up in here," the woman said, "and gag them. That way, even if the cops knock on the door, the kids won't be able to respond. The other apartments are empty; if there's no response when someone knocks here, they'll assume this one is vacant, too."

Cat Burglar on the Prowl

"No need to gag them," the man said. "I can fix it so they don't make any noise. Last thing, just before we leave, I'll take care of it." He looked at Rosie and Kayo. His mouth smiled, but his eyes did not.

"You're disgusting, Ed. You know that?" the woman said. "I think you're actually looking forward to this."

They gathered up another load and left, without saying anything to the girls.

Chapter

*T*he room was nearly empty.

"There isn't much left," Rosie said. "The next load will be their last."

"If we don't do something fast," Kayo said, "he's going to come back in here and turn our lights out. When he's finished with us, we'll be lucky if we can ever lift a bat—or a pencil—again."

"Do you really think she will stand there and watch him whack us around?" Rosie said.

"Whether she watches or not, it will feel the same."

"Even if she won't let him hurt us, we'll be tied and gagged and locked in here while they go free. It might be days before our notes are found. Weeks, even! Or they might never be found."

"I'm scared," Kayo said.

"So am I. If our notes aren't found, we could be here until someone wants to rent this apartment."

"By then," said Kayo, "we might be nothing but a pile of bones."

Rosie nodded. "And all the people like you that they stole from would never get their things back."

Kayo thought about her mother, crying for her silver tea set. She remembered the awful, cold fear that had kept her and her mom from sleeping in their own home.

If the cat burglar got away now, what would stop him from going to her home again? Even if she and Rosie were rescued, she would live in fear that he might return.

"I don't know about you," Kayo said, "but I am not willing to stand here like a brainless Barbie doll and do nothing but wait for him to come back and knock us senseless."

"I'm not going to fight them," Rosie said. "That would not be smart. He would just get angrier than he is already and be all the harder on us."

Kayo took the Mickey Mantle baseball out

from under her cap and turned it over and over in her hand. Rage made her blood run faster.

"He is the most horrible man I have ever seen," Rosie said. "And he's so big!"

"Bigger," Kayo said slowly, "isn't necessarily smarter."

"What are you thinking?"

"I have a game plan."

"What is it?"

Kayo explained quickly.

"It might work," Rosie said.

"Hurry!" Kayo said. "We have to be in position when they return."

Rosie grabbed Webster's cage and set it on the floor where it would be behind the door when the door opened. She crouched beside the cage and opened the latch. Webster flattened his ears. His tail swished back and forth like a windshield wiper.

Kayo rushed to the back corner of the room, opposite the door. She started a practice windup, as if she were pitching.

"Whatever happens," Rosie said, "you will always be my best friend."

Kayo stopped in the middle of her windup. Just when the world was blackest, Rosie's words shone like a flashlight, chasing the shadows. She looked at Rosie's round face, framed by short brown hair, and Rosie's brown eyes behind her glasses. Kayo knew she was lucky to have such a friend.

"Thanks," Kayo said. "You're my best friend, too." This plan had better work, she thought, because if it doesn't and that awful man hurts Rosie, it will be all my fault for suggesting that Care Club enter the cat show, and I will never forgive myself. Never!

"Here they come," Rosie whispered. "Get ready."

The key turned in the lock.

Rosie put both hands in the cage.

Kayo pounded the Mickey Mantle baseball into her palm.

The door opened.

Rosie dragged Webster out of the cage.

The woman came in.

Rosie leaped from behind the door. Both girls screamed as loudly as they could, and Rosie tossed a yowling Webster toward the startled woman.

Webster clung to the woman's shoulder, digging in his claws. He hissed and spit.

The woman shrieked and tried to push Webster off.

Webster bit the woman's hand. The woman dropped her keys.

"Get off! Get off!" the woman screeched.

Rosie bent down and snatched the keys.

"Ed!" the woman yelled. "Get this wild animal off me!"

Kayo went into her windup.

The man dropped the handle of the cart in the hallway and rushed into the room. As he grabbed for Webster, Kayo threw her best fastball.

It hit the man right in the stomach.

"Uummph!" he said and dropped to the floor.

"Run!" yelled Rosie as she bolted out the door.

Chapter

13

"Ed!" the woman shrieked. "Get up and help me!"

Webster climbed from the woman's shoulder to her head, leaving deep red scratches in the woman's cheek. He stood on the woman's hair, his tail pointing straight up and his back humped like a camel. His fur stuck out in all directions, his teeth showed, and an ominous growl came from deep in his throat.

When Ed didn't respond, the woman reached up to push Webster off. Webster slashed at her hand, claws out.

Kayo dashed across the room as the man struggled to sit up.

He leaned on one elbow, holding his stomach and gasping for breath.

Kayo sidestepped him easily and made it out the door, slamming it shut behind her.

"I nailed him right in the bread basket," Kayo said. "Knocked the wind out of him, but good."

From inside the door the woman bellowed, "Help! Get this wild animal off me."

"Hang on, Webster," muttered Kayo.

Rosie stuck the key in the lock and turned it, locking the man and woman inside. "I hate to leave Webster in there with those two crooks," she said as she started down the stairs.

"Webster is evening the score," Kayo replied.

They ran downstairs and pounded on Mrs. Watson's door. The door opened a crack.

"We need to use your telephone," Rosie said.

"Did you find your hat?" Mrs. Watson said.

Kayo put her hand to her ear, as if she were holding a telephone receiver. "Police," she yelled. "We need to call the police. *Police!*"

Mrs. Watson smiled, nodded, and opened the door. "It's nice to hear you say please," she said. "So many young people these days have no manners."

Rosie dashed to the telephone and dialed 911.

"We've captured the cat burglar," she said. "He stole my cat and we found him and—"

"Is this the same girl who called earlier about a stolen cat?" the operator said.

"We caught him," Rosie said.

"I told you before not to tie up an emergency line over a cat."

"He has a whole van full of stolen TVs and stereos and jewelry," Rosie said.

"Who does?"

"The cat burglar! I just told you, we've caught the cat burglar. We caught his partner, too."

"Where is he?" the operator said. "What's the address?"

Rosie turned to Mrs. Watson. "What's your address?" she asked.

"Thank you. I've always liked this dress, too."

"House number," Rosie said. "What's your house number?"

"Come again, dear?"

Kayo ran outside, looked at the house number, and returned.

Minutes later the police arrived. While one officer took Rosie's and Kayo's name and phone number, two other officers quickly examined the blue van filled with stolen merchandise. Then the girls led the police upstairs to the end apartment and handed over the keys to the door.

"You girls go downstairs," an officer said. "We don't want anyone getting hurt."

"But Webster is in there. He'll be terrified until he sees me again."

Kayo gaped at Rosie. She couldn't believe Rosie was arguing with a police officer.

The officer stood firm, ordering Rosie to follow Kayo down the stairs.

They crouched on the steps, partway to the second floor, where they could hear what was said.

The police pounded on the door and shouted, "Drop your weapons and come out with your hands up."

Rosie and Kayo crept far enough up the stairs so they could see down the hall and into the last apartment.

The police unlocked the door, flung it open, and yelled, "Stay where you are."

When the door opened, Webster dashed out the door. He streaked between the officers' legs, and ran down the steps straight into Rosie's arms. Rosie held him tight. "It's okay," she whispered. "You're safe now. We're going to take you home."

Webster burrowed his head into the crook of Rosie's arm and cuddled close.

"They're gone!" A police officer called out. "The place is empty."

Cat Burglar on the Prowl

Kayo and Rosie looked at each other in disbelief for a second, and then, exactly at the same time, they said, "The roof!"

They dashed up the stairs. Webster got scared when Rosie ran, and he tried to jump out of her arms. By the time they got inside the apartment, the police had already discovered the broken window and two of them had jumped down to the roof.

Kayo rushed to the window and looked down. Rosie quickly put Webster in his cage and then joined Kayo at the window in time to hear the police tell the man and woman their rights.

The woman barely listened. She kept rubbing the top of her head and then examining her fingers, as if expecting to find blood.

The police officer climbed back in the window first, followed by the woman. As soon as she was in the room, an officer slapped handcuffs on her.

"We almost made it," the woman said. "If Ed wasn't so stupid, we would have cleared five grand this month."

At the sound of the woman's voice, Webster pressed his face against the side of his cage and growled.

"Get that beast out of here," the woman said.

The cat burglar climbed in the window, followed by the second police officer. The cat burglar swore as the handcuffs were clamped on him. He glared at Rosie and Kayo. "I should have taken care of you two when I had the chance," he snarled.

Kayo shuddered, realizing how close they had come to real disaster.

Rosie picked up Webster's cage.

"You stole my great-grandmother's silver tea set," Kayo said, "and I want it back."

"I never saw any tea set," the man said.

"Neither did I," said the woman.

"If they have it," said one of the police officers, "we'll find it."

"My mom really is a lawyer," Rosie said as she and Kayo headed for the door.

The woman groaned.

"But we lied to you about the cat," Kayo said. "This cat is the Grand Champion."

"That's right," said Rosie. "Grand Champion Webster."

"You see?" said the man to the woman. "I told you so, but you wouldn't believe me."

The girls made it all the way down the stairs to the first floor before they doubled over with laughter.

As a police officer drove them back to the school to meet Mrs. Benton, Kayo said, "The cat show was a great Care Club project, even if we didn't win any money for the homeless animals."

Cat Burglar on the Prowl

"By catching the cat burglar, we made a difference in the lives of a lot of people," Rosie said. "And Webster seemed to like hanging on to that woman's hair."

"I wonder what my mom and your parents will say when they hear that we caught the cat burglar."

"Maybe they'll say we're ineffable," Rosie said. She stopped to make a check mark in her notebook. "That's five times today," she said with satisfaction.

"Ineffable?" said Kayo. "That's what you said about Sweet Sapphire's price. I thought it meant expensive."

"You," said Rosie, "will never have a decent vocabulary."

Chapter

14

"Get over here right away," Kayo shouted into the telephone. "We need an emergency Care Club meeting."

"For what?"

"I'll tell you when you get here. Hurry!"

Ten minutes later Rosie and Kayo sat on Kayo's bed, with the bedroom door shut.

"The Care Club meeting will now come to order," Kayo said.

"This had better be good," Rosie said. "My mother was taking cinnamon rolls out of the oven when you called."

"I have called this emergency meeting," Kayo said, "because Care Club has some important business that will make a huge difference in the lives of homeless animals."

"Forget it," said Rosie. "I'm not ready for another project. I haven't recovered from the cat show yet and neither has Webster. He wouldn't even eat his crunchies last night."

"Is there any unfinished business?" Kayo said.

To Kayo's surprise, Rosie said, "Yes."

"There is?"

"When I told my parents how Mrs. Watson can't hear, they arranged to get hearing aids for her." Rosie opened her dictionary and started paging through it.

Kayo wasn't sure Mrs. Watson's hearing aids qualified as Care Club business, but she was happy to know about it.

"Kayo?" Mrs. Benton called up the stairs. "There's someone here to see you."

"I'll wait here," Rosie said as she paged through the dictionary. "I need to find a word for next week."

A few minutes later Kayo stomped into the room. "You and your bright ideas," she said.

"What did I do?"

"That was Sammy Hulenback." She threw a folded piece of paper into the wastebasket.

"He actually did it?" Rosie said. "He wrote you a love poem?"

"Could we please get on with the meeting?" Kayo said.

"What does it say?"

"I didn't read it."

Rosie dropped the dictionary and reached into the wastebasket. She unfolded the paper. "It *is* a poem," she said. She read aloud:

"Kayo has such pretty eyes,
And she's good at catching flies."

Rosie stopped reading and looked at Kayo. "First a squirrel," she said, "and now flies. He *is* weird."

"He means fly balls," said Kayo.

"Oh." Rosie read the rest of the poem.

"Her hair is blond and not too curly.
She's a very pretty girlie.

"Girlie?" Kayo said. "He called me a *girlie?*"

Rosie nodded and held out the poem.

"Yuck!" cried Kayo. "I think I'm going to throw up." She grabbed the poem, crumpled it into a ball, and threw it back in the wastebasket.

Rosie snatched it out and started smoothing the paper.

"What are you doing?" Kayo said.

"This is your very first love letter," Rosie said. "You should keep it. After you're inducted into the Baseball Hall of Fame, things like this will be valuable."

Kayo put her hands on her hips. "Tear it up," she ordered.

"Wouldn't you like to have a copy of Joe DiMaggio's first love letter?"

"No," said Kayo. "Not if it was as stupid as this one."

"I'm probably tearing up a hundred dollars' worth of sports memorabilia," Rosie said. But she ripped the poem to shreds.

"If there is no more unfinished business," Kayo said, "we'll go on to the treasurer's report."

"Since Care Club did not win First Place in the cat show," Rosie said, "we are still broke, the same as last meeting."

"We won't be, by this time tomorrow," Kayo said.

Rosie gave her a suspicious look.

"Tomorrow afternoon," Kayo continued, "Care Club will have not one hundred but *two* hundred dollars!"

Rosie leaned close and whispered, "You didn't keep that Mickey Mantle baseball and sell it, did you?"

"Of course not," Kayo said. "I would never sell

a baseball autographed by Mickey Mantle. Not if I was orphaned and starving and needed an operation on my pitching arm. Never! Never, never, never!"

"All right, all right," said Rosie.

"I left the baseball in the apartment, for the police."

"Then where are we getting two hundred dollars?"

"There was a reward! A woman whose house was robbed offered a two-hundred-dollar reward for information leading to the arrest of the cat burglar."

"And we provided the information," said Rosie.

"Someone from the police department called my mom just before I called you. They found her silver tea set in one of the pillowcases, and they also told her about the reward. We can go down tomorrow afternoon and pick up the tea set and a check. We're rich!" Visions of the new baseball glove floated in Kayo's mind.

"So this emergency meeting is to decide what to do with the money," Rosie said.

"That's right," Kayo said. "I thought we could give The Humane Society one hundred dollars to groom the dogs and make them smell good, just like we planned to do if we had won first prize

112

in the cat show. And the other hundred ." She could almost feel that new glove on her hand.

"The other hundred," Rosie said, "can buy food for the homeless animals."

Kayo sighed.

"Think of all the hungry animals this much money will feed," Rosie said. "Care Club finally lived up to its charter."

Kayo imagined bowls of food being placed in front of homeless puppies and kittens. Maybe a new baseball glove wasn't so important, after all. She smiled at Rosie.

"My joy," said Kayo, "is ineffable."

"There's hope for you yet," said Rosie.

About the Author

Peg Kehret lives with her husband, Carl, and their animal friends in an old farmhouse in Washington State. They have two grown children and four grandchildren. They enjoy traveling throughout the U.S., where Peg speaks at schools, sharing her enthusiasm for books and writing.

Peg's popular novels for young people frequently appear on award lists. Her Minstrel titles include *Horror at the Haunted House; Nightmare Mountain* (Nebraska Golden Sower Award, Young Hoosier Book Award, West Virginia Children's Book Award Honor Book, Iowa Children's Choice Award, International Reading Association Children's Book Council Children's Choice); *Sisters, Long Ago* (International Reading Association Young Adults' Choice); *Cages* (an ALA Recommended Book for Reluctant Readers, International Reading Association Young Adults' Choice); *Terror at the Zoo* (International Reading Association Young Adults' Choice); and her forthcoming series, *Frightmares*.